The Teeny Tiny

GHOST

and the

MONSTER

by Kay Winters
illustrated by Lynn Munsinger

HarperCollins*Publishers*

"Listen up!" said the teacher
to the teeny tiny class.
"The Spook and Spirit Club
is sponsoring a contest
for all the ghosts
in our teeny tiny school."

"A contest?"
squeaked the timid teeny tiny ghost.
"It's a Make a Monster contest—
just in time for Halloween.
They are looking for a monster
that no one has ever seen!"
said the teeny tiny teacher with a great big grin.
"Yay!" cheered the ghosts
in the teeny tiny class.

Then they shouted their ideas
one by one.
"A monster that is hairy!
One that you'd be scared to meet."

"A monster that is fierce, with fangs,
and has too many feet."

"And one that gobbles girls for breakfast,
boys for lunch,
and *cats* for trick or treat,"
added Buster with a Big Bad Grin.
"Oh no," cried the timid teeny tiny ghost.
He sat up very straight
in his teeny tiny seat
and clutched his teeny tiny black cats.

With big black markers,
and paint as red as blood,
the little ghosts in the class
began to draw.
But the teeny tiny ghost
put his teeny tiny head
down on his teeny tiny desk.

How could he make a monster
that was horrible and hairy?
That would be much too scary,
like a nightmare coming true.

"What a wimp!" whispered Wilma.
"What a teeny tiny twerp."
"He's a baby," mocked Buster
in a whiny baby voice.
"Goo goo
       boo-hoo,
            Baby boo!"

He shot a rubber band
at the teeny tiny ghost.

"Time's up," said the teacher
as she put away the paints.
"Take your monsters home with you
and finish them tonight.
Tomorrow we will hang them all
and give ourselves a fright."

"Where's yours?" whispered Wilma
to the teeny tiny ghost.
"Didn't do it?
Too bad.
Bet the teacher will be mad.
You're the *only one*
who won't be in the contest."

"Don't give up. Never quit!"
said the teeny tiny teacher
as she hugged
the timid teeny tiny ghost.
"I know you can do it
if you put your mind to it,"
she whispered in his teeny tiny ear.

The teeny tiny ghost
sighed a teeny tiny sigh
and picked up his two black cats.
Then they started flying home
over teeny tiny town.

But Buster and Wilma
flew right behind them.
Diving in, diving out,
up and over,
round about,
till the teeny tiny ghost felt dizzy.

Down, down he flew

to the teeny tiny dump,
and hid underneath an old clock.

"Soccer practice!" shouted Wilma
as she looked at her watch.
"Buster! We'll be late! It's time to go!"
"Bye-bye, Baby boo!"
Buster called as they flew.
And they zoomed off to the teeny tiny park.

"Phew!" said the teeny tiny ghost.
"They're gone!"
And he and his cats looked around.
There were raggy, saggy sofas,
springs and wires out of place,
and a teeny tiny clock
with one hand upon his face.

There were checkers
but no game boards.
No brooms
but lots of mops.
There were cages but no songbirds.
There were cartons with no tops.

The teeny tiny ghost gave a teeny tiny giggle
as he saw what his cats had in mind.
"Here's a monster in the making!
We can do this after all."

The teeny tiny ghost
found bits and pieces that he wanted.
He stacked them
and he packed them
in a box without a lid
and flew home to his teeny tiny house.

All afternoon, till the moon rode high,
the teeny tiny ghost and his teeny tiny cats
worked in his teeny tiny barn.

He drilled and they hammered
with a *rap! rap! rap!*
He poked and they pounded
with a *tap! tap! tap!*
He twisted and they turned
the wires tight in place.
Then the teeny tiny ghost
finally made his monster's face.

On Halloween morning
at teeny tiny school
some very scary creatures
peered down from the wall.
"That's mine," boasted Buster.
"It's the meanest one of all."

When the teeny tiny ghost
and his cats flew in,
they pulled and pushed their monster
down the hall.
Monster bounced on its springs
with a *BIM*

      BAM

          BOING!

The teeny tiny ghost
took a teeny tiny bow.
"I made a friendly monster
out of parts from the dump.
It can stand.
It can *B-O-I-N-G.*
It makes me laugh!"

Buster smirked. Wilma snickered.
And then Buster spoke,
very softly so the teacher wouldn't hear.
"Who ever heard of a monster
made of parts from the dump?
It wouldn't scare a baby.
It's a teeny tiny chump!"

All morning *l* . . . *o* . . . *n* . . . *g*
the teeny tiny ghosts
wondered who would win the Monster contest.
They wiggled. They giggled.
They couldn't keep still.

At recess the teeny tiny teacher
stood guard by the teeny tiny door.
No one could peek!
At last she jangled her teeny tiny bell.

The teeny tiny ghosts lined up to go inside.
Then they marched to the teeny tiny hall.
There were bright satin ribbons
from the Spook and Spirit Club.

Yellow for the monster
whose eyes glared and glittered.
Red for the one with the lips
that snarled and sneered.
But the big blue ribbon—
the prize for being best,
and never seen before—
was on the friendly monster's chest.

Clap clap clap . . . Clap clap clap
sounded up and down the hall.
Was some of that clapping
from the monsters on the wall?
The teeny tiny ghost gave a big thumbs-up
and beamed at his two black cats.
"I knew we could do it
if we put our minds to it!
And we won the blue ribbon
after all!"

To Oliver, who loves the Teeny Tiny Ghost!
—K.W.

For the children of Greenfield
—L.M.

The Teeny Tiny Ghost and the Monster
Text copyright © 2004 by Kay Winters
Illustrations copyright © 2004 by Lynn Munsinger
Manufactured in China. All rights reserved. No part of this book may be used
or reproduced in any manner whatsoever without written permission except in the case
of brief quotations embodied in critical articles and reviews. For information address
HarperCollins Children's Books, a division of HarperCollins Publishers,
1350 Avenue of the Americas, New York, NY 10019.
www.harperchildrens.com

Library of Congress Cataloging-in-Publication Data
Winters, Kay.
 The teeny tiny ghost and the monster / by Kay Winters ; illustrated by Lynn Munsinger.
   p.   cm.
 Summary: The teeny tiny ghost and his classmates enter a monster-making contest at their
school.
 ISBN-10: 0-06-028884-1 (trade bdg.) — ISBN-13: 978-0-06-028884-6 (trade bdg.)
 ISBN-10: 0-06-028885-X (lib. bdg.) — ISBN-13: 978-0-06-028885-3 (lib. bdg.)
 ISBN-10: 0-06-443662-4 (pbk.) — ISBN-13: 978-0-06-443662-5 (pbk.)
 [1. Ghosts—Fiction. 2. Monsters—Fiction. 3. Contests—Fiction. 4. Schools—Fiction.]
I. Munsinger, Lynn, ill. II. Title.
PZ7.W7675 Ti 2004
[E]—dc21   2002010501
                                                                      CIP
                                                                       AC

Typography by Elynn Cohen ❖ First Edition